The Chemical Choir

Written By:
Brandon Lamarque Farley

ISBN

Hardcover: 978-1-966902-25-6
Paperback: 978-1-966902-26-3

Dedication

Hey guys, I'd like to dedicate this remarkable book to all my precious loved ones, who help me prepare for my remarkable future, life, and more. I have been very happily enjoying living with them that keeps me interested in enjoying living my remarkable life of mines and that also keeps me uplifted with strength and dignity within me, just precisely like I'm pretty sure that I do for them also as well guys, because I've always held onto and remembered all of the very beautiful words and things that they have always said to me, such as, my beautiful mother and father, children, grandmother and grandfather, and of course my sweet gorgeous beautiful girlfriend of mines, Mrs. Shantay Marie Cohens, that has always kept me uplifted and invigorated within my spirit and body to carry on guys.

Acknowledgement

Hi, everyone, I'd like to acknowledge my beautiful mother and father, as well as my beautiful girlfriend and my kids, just to name a few, including myself. Who kept me strengthened and uplifted to carry on enjoying my life, my homie.

About the Author

Hi, guys. I'm going to be a small-town, laid-back Cherokee Indian country boy from Brighton, GA. Named Brandon Lamarque Farley, where I grew up surrounded by friends and remarkable family members of mine who always kept me strong and uplifted to carry on enjoying living my life, homie. Thank you.

Chapter 1

This is the story of Kiara Johnson, Latonia Renee Woodard, Shantay Cohens, and Brandon Lamarque Farley. Even though all three women lived entirely different lives, they still all had something in common. They all had "him." This was something really very special and incredible to have. You see, all three women had dated him once before. The fact that Brandon was known to date many girls never diminished the love each couple shared. But, Brandon had a particular eye out for a certain someone named Kiara Johnson.

Yep, you heard me right; Homeboy sure did have a liking for that girl right there. When they had met each other, they had screwed each other on the first night, but it still never diminished the love brewing between them. Brandon Lamarque Farley was a stunner. Kiara was enraptured by his looks and could not take her eyes of him the first time they had met. When he very first saw her and laid eyes on her as she stood on the dance floor of Apple Bee's studio, he knew he needed her in his life. The beautiful, unique, designed African American young lady named Kiara Johnson captured his heart.

One day, on a special night out that Brandon likes to call a night out on the prowl, something marvelous took place. He randomly stumbled upon a beautiful young lady. It was as if a bow was pointed at him and an arrow was shot at his heart. He could not believe that such a stunner was right before his eyes.

He had to pry his gaze away from her for a while as he had work to do. But, once he secured his package, he made his way back to her eagerly. He danced the night away with her, and after that, he never let her go.

Anyone in the room could tell that those two had intense chemistry. There was something special brewing between them that night. It was a moment of magic on the dancefloor.

As he danced, Brandon felt he was so on point. He was dancing rhythmically to the beats, his heart was racing, and his adrenaline was pumping. It was the biggest adrenaline rush of his life; the kind that would take your breath away and have you soaring to new heights that one could only dream of. He knew he had to react quickly and keep his balance. On that dance floor on that night, he was falling in love.

He got the chance to fall in love with a very special someone like that. As if it was nothing at all to him, he fell in love with this very special young lady, y'all.

It was in the middle of the night, on one of the darkest, most random, wild nights he had ever had. It was so stunningly dazzling, bewildering, and beautiful that it could completely steal your focus and leave you standing there in a bizarre, paralyzed, beast-like stupor, staring with all eyes fixed on the girl before you. It was the kind of random, bizarre, special night where, if you weren't careful, you could lose yourself in an instant—in the blink of an eye.

That was when Brandon found himself holding on to all his prized Cherokee Indian possessions and more. I had to tell Brandon Farley myself when I saw him, "Ouuuuwee, you go, boy, because you sure do got it going on! Old boy, I sure do wish I could be you, standing up there dancing the night away with that beautiful, special young lady of yours, old boy!"

He never heard me because he was too busy being all caught up with Kiara Johnson and all. Boy, lemme tell ya, he sure did have a liking for that girl right there, but what people didn't know was that this amazing, good-looking young guy right there who was standing there paralyzed. He was standing there half-ass stuck himself dancing with Kiara Johnson in the midst of all of her friends, and he was very nervous about the whole thing. It was something that would leave anyone stuck there stammering, shivering, and just shaking if you weren't like Brandon Lamarque Farley is y'all. But you wouldn't have been able to tell that he was going through all of that from the reassuring look on his face. Standing all alone, right up there on the dance floor with her y'all, he was like a deer caught up in some high-beam headlights. They were headlights that would blind ya and kill ya as soon as possible.

As Bradon Lamarque Farley approached her, she was standing out there on the dance floor with all of her girlfriends. He approached her in a very quick, kind, gentle, respectful kind of way. His manner would leave you stunned, saying, "I don't like this shit right here at mother fucking all," or "I'm either going to go right along with all this bullshit or not." This was because he was one of those types of guys that you would either run away from or run away with. He was the type of guy who had to say to anyone, "Ahh, you don't have to be worried so much about me." But in fact, it could be just the total opposite because you could get caught up in a run-in with this guy who would leave your tail tucked between your legs. If you caught this guy on a bad day when he wasn't feeling good, boy, he sure would show nuff and run you away from him.

Ya see, he comes from that race of mythological myths called Cherokees—Indians who could leave you stuck standing still, gazing off in the other direction while he's working on ya. All the while, you'd be hoping he'd let you go, yet there you'd stay, paralyzed by him. Stuck staring straight into his gaze—or not—that would leave anyone wondering: "Oh, why did I do this? How did I get myself into this mess with him? And Lord, when is this mother fucker right here going to let me go? Also, what is he going to do next?"

See, Brandon was just that exotic. He was just that special. Everybody always knew to move right out of his way when they saw him coming through. Ya see, because Brandon didn't play around. He had that special kind of allure that could get anybody or anything up off of him and leave you paralyzed if you weren't careful.

"So, what's everybody standing around for?" said Brandon. "Come on, move it along now, let's go."

And they had every single reason to be worried about him, y'all, because he was just that incredibly gifted and alarmingly dangerous. A young Cherokee Indian man who was a threat to all his foes if anyone ever tried to step out of line with him or his loved ones, that is.

"Ya see, because it would be me you'd be dealing with if anyone ever stepped out of line with me or my loved ones. And I'm no amateur," said Brandon.

It was on the dance floor, as he grabbed her waist, that Brandon found himself stammering, caught off guard, stuttering, and shakily acknowledging her. He was shaken up, trying to figure out just the right words to say to score with her, shooting his shot. Even though he was rattled, caught up in the moment, he didn't let it scare him off. He pushed ahead, y'all, because he knew just a little something about the situation he was caught in.

See, Brandon was a stallion among stallions—someone who could move through any crowd, any wave, even vultures and more.

Like a compass, he guided himself and her through all the bull crap they were caught up in with ease. Once everything started to level out and flow smoothly to the rhythm of his beat, he found himself flowing with her, like a wave crashing onto the beach.

Ya see, he could see straight through it all—enough to get them both out of the wilderness, as soft as clouds passing over an open lake. As Brandon slowly regained his composure, he realized he was getting exactly what he came for. He knew he couldn't seem too suspicious or off-putting around this girl because if he had, he'd have lost her. But he didn't, y'all.

You see, Brandon Lamarque Farley was a gentleman among gentlemen and a stallion among stallions, who stood out maturely and ranked high among his peers. As he held her close, accomplishing the goals laid before him like a destiny he didn't even realize at first, he moved through it all so elegantly with her. Speaking to her empathetically, Brandon sent out all the right signals in a way that anyone would buy, bite, or try to hold onto.

In his uniquely special way, with his beautiful violin-like voice that could hit any note or pitch just right, sending shockwaves through you, disarming you completely, he said, "Oh, come on now, girl. Don't push me away, old girl."

Brandon said this to Kiara Johnson as she stood there, pinched in the back of the crowd with her girlfriends. When she sighed and turned back away from him, acting as though nothing had happened between them, boy, it was like magic, y'all. As Brandon started to calm down, realizing he was safe and in good hands, he let his guard down. He had secured the prize and cleared the night away, walking out with a thick, beautiful reward: someone he would spend the rest of his life with, someone who was never boring to him.

Even through all the bullshit and challenges they faced together, they held onto each other and never let go—like Jack in *Titanic*, y'all. They endured it all with bemused good humor, and from the way Brandon handled everything that night, she knew she was safe and in very good hands. He protected them from all the bullshit.

As time passed, they shared many adventurous adventures, journeys, time, tours, assignments, arguments, discussions, love making and more together y'all. Comfort, peace, and security defined their years together—time that flew by because they were always caught up in each other, enjoying what they loved most. That was really something y'all.

To Brandon, it felt like nothing else mattered except the good times they shared. This beautiful young lady, Kiara Johnson, who he'd never met before that night but later learned had been tailing him, became his world. The connection they shared made everything else fade into the background. They knew just enough about each other to secure their connection, y'all. Nothing else in the world mattered to them except their well-being and the life they built together.

To Brandon, it seemed like time flew by both alarmingly fast and slow. He never had to worry about anything because he was always caught up in Kiara's warm embrace, wrapped in her presence like a cocoon of safety and love. As time passed, they moved through life together, enveloped in a halo of peace, as if nothing could touch them or disrupt their harmony. It was as soft as clouds moving over an open lake, filling the empty spaces of life. That sense of peace made them dream of a future together—maybe getting married, having kids, or just building a life filled with the things they loved most. You know how it is when people start planning their lives with someone they love, right y'all?

Now, Brandon was a handful. Some folks might've called him a rambunctious loose cannon, a sword ready to strike, or worse. Some people might even call him a dumb black ugly, looking mother fucking god damn son of a bitch because Gee-whiz, the mother freaking guy, was just that great. But, he was so well covered defensively because, boy, that guy right there really sure could keep you up off of him and his loved ones, like a mother fucker; he didn't play when it came to his family, his values, or the things he held dear. A proud Cherokee Indian man, he carried himself with confidence and knew how to defend what mattered most.

Brandon Lamarque Farley knew how to live his life. He had a way of enjoying himself with whomever he wanted, without too much confrontation, because he handled situations like that very well. Let me give you a brief, detailed, and historically oriented-background about this man right here, y'all.

It took real guts for him to walk across that dance floor to ask Kiara Johnson to dance with him that night. He didn't know what would happen or that they'd wind up falling in love and starting a relationship together. All he knew, as they stood there sharing so much with each other, was that he was in good hands. Boy, he really liked that girl, y'all.

Brandon was a handful, no doubt about it. He was an incredibly bright, intelligent young Cherokee Indian gentleman. He had this glow about him—so much so that the ladies couldn't keep their hands off him. And the gentlemen? Well, they didn't want to mess with him either because he could defend himself just fine.

He was a cultivated gentleman—a man of high virtues as a husband, father, and citizen. A true standup guy. To him, that was the highest honor a man could have. His life was filled with events some might call miracles, homie, and for him, it was all worth it. Swell.

Brandon really did know how to enjoy life. He lived on his terms, choosing whom to share it with, and he had this special ability to make everyone around him feel seen and valued. It didn't bother him one bit if people were jealous of his life or his way of carrying himself. He carried on a legacy of his own, loving his family and friends fiercely while defending his honor and enjoying life to the fullest.

Despite his charm and effortless way of winning people over, he still faced challenges. No matter how difficult something seemed to others, it was nothing to him. You see, Brandon had a unique way of disarming people without them even realizing it. By the time they figured it out, he was already on his way, handling his business.

"Man, he always had that about him," someone once said.

He never took advantage of anyone, not once. But people often tried to take advantage of him. None of them succeeded, though— not a single one. Brandon stood his ground, a skill he learned from his father and others who helped shape him.

This young Cherokee Indian gentleman wasn't just cultivated— he could rumble when necessary, too. Maybe that's why he got along with so many people while still managing to navigate his way out of anything that came his way.

That's what made him so special. I don't know about you, but I sure wouldn't mind getting to know someone like that, y'all.

As time moved on in this young gentleman's life, he ventured out on what he liked to call "a night out on the prowl, y'all." Leaving his mother's house that evening, he had no idea what to expect. He rambled on, having an enjoyable conversation with himself about life and its many musings—not really looking for anything in particular, but still managing to find something extraordinary.

That's when he met her: Kiara Johnson, his beautiful African girl. It all happened so naturally, almost as if it were meant to be. They danced the night away after he bumped into her, standing there with her girlfriends on the dance floor at one of America's Applebee's club nights. Yes, you heard that right—Applebee's, y'all. That's where it all began.

She stood there, uniquely special, her presence radiating something he couldn't quite put into words. Maybe she was wondering the same thing he was—something along the lines of, "Oouu, what in the fuck am I even must doing here out here tonight y'all. With hardly shit going on in my life." She seemed almost hidden in the crowd as if she didn't want to be noticed, and yet, somehow, he found her.

And for all he knew, she bumped right back into him too—like the mother fucking god damn queen. As he approached her, moving through the crowd with a smooth elegance, he started dancing with her, catching her off guard in the best way possible.

Her girlfriends took notice. Kiara glanced back at them, saying, "Hey y'all, come here and check this out. Girl, who is this fine, gorgeous, handsome young man dancing with me out here on the floor tonight?"

One of her friends responded, "I don't know, for all we know, somebody who just wants to get to know you hell."

When they figured out who he was, their voices harmonized, "Oh, that's Brandon Farley! Girl, he's alright. He's one of them country boys from Brighton. Yeah, he's a good man. Go ahead and dance with him—try to get to know him if you can."

With their approval, Kiara turned back around, giving Brandon one of her sexy, playful glares that said everything without saying a word. To him, it felt like he was treading on thin ice, almost as if he could've lost her before he even had her.

But he didn't.

This big, beautiful, thick, gorgeous African American woman had found her match that night. She gave him one last playful look that spoke volumes, and he responded with one of his casual, confident, signature smiles as if to say, *"Aw, come on now, don't push me away."*

She let out a small *"Hmph"* before turning back around and continuing to dance with him. And together, they danced the night away.

The End.

(With more to come.)